Merry Christmas.
Love you very much!
Grandma ☺"

Wonky Donkey's
BIG Surprise

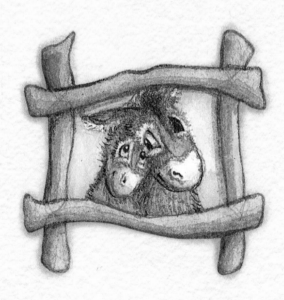

This book is dedicated to all those parents (my mum included)
who are away from their families, often in the service of
their wider community. When sacrificing your time away,
you not only protect your family but our families too.
Thank you, from the bottom of my heart.
– Craig Smith

For my precious mama, for your wisdom and innocence, curiosity
and knowing, playfulness and depth . . . and for teaching me the
beauty of falling about laughing, and loving, no matter what.
May these qualities ripple out into the world to pave the way to
a wonderful future for our new souls coming through.
– Katz Cowley

whiffy: stinky

Library of Congress Cataloging-in-Publication Data available

ISBN 978-1-338-77999-8

10 9 8 7 6 5 4 3 2 1   21 22 23 24 25

Printed in the U.S.A. 40
This edition first printing, November 2021

The artwork was created using watercolor and colored pencil.
The text was set in Drawzing.

Book design by Smartwork Creative Ltd, www.smartworkcreative.co.nz

Wonky Donkey's
BIG Surprise

Words by Craig Smith
Illustrations by Katz Cowley

SCHOLASTIC INC.
NEW YORK TORONTO LONDON AUCKLAND
SYDNEY MEXICO CITY NEW DELHI HONG KONG

Dinky woke one weekend
with wonder in her eyes.
Today her daddy, Wonky, promised
such a big surprise.

What could it be? she wondered
as she jumped up with a bray.

Hee Haw!

She was feeling so excited
on this very special day.

She asked her dad to tell her;
she couldn't stand the stress.
But Wonky said he wouldn't,
though she could try and guess!

"Take a seat," said Wonky,
"here on the stable floor."
Then he explained that her surprise
was behind the big green door.

"Oh, I love this guessing game!"
with a smile, Dinky said.
What could it be, *this big surprise?*
Many thoughts ran through her head.

She knew she'd been a good girl.
Well, perhaps . . . more or less.
She deserved a special present,
but first she'd try and guess.

"Is it warm?" asked Dinky.

"Very warm," said Wonky Donkey.

"Is it washable?"

"It washes itself."

"Does it have whiskers?"

"Yes, but we don't mention that."

"This surprise sounds weird!"

"Yes, but all the good ones are."

"Is it witty?"

"Ha ha, you'll laugh and laugh!"

"Does it wiggle?"

"Only when tickled."

"Is it wise?"

"Very, very wise."

"Is it wrinkly?"

"Hmm . . . I've never noticed."

"Is it ... wonderful?"

"It's the most wonderful thing
in the whole wide world!"

"Wait ... is it whiffy too?"

Hee Hee Haw!

"Sometimes it's even whiffier
than your dad!"

Dinky could wait no longer!
She leapt up from the floor.
She knew what her surprise was
behind that big green door!

She knew of only ONE thing that was
wonderful, wrinkly,
        wiggly, witty, weird,
            whiskery, washable,
                warm, whiffy, and wise.

Dinky pulled the door wide open
to see Wonky's big surprise . . .

And the warmth flowed
through her as she
met with familiar
eyes . . .